THERE ONCE WAS
A
DOG

THERE ONCE WAS A
DOG

Adélia Carvalho • João Vaz de Carvalho

North South

Daddy, Daddy, tell me a story!
There once was an alligator with only one foot. . . .
Not the alligator. Oh, no! I want the dog story instead.
I'm afraid I don't know that one.

There once was a lion that had a great itch.
Not the lion. Oh, no! I want the dog story instead.
I'm afraid I don't know that one.

There once was a pig with a wonky snout.
Not the pig. Oh, no! I want the dog story instead.
I'm afraid I don't know that one.

There once was a hen that hatched an idea.
Not the hen. Oh, no! I want the dog story instead.
I'm afraid I don't know that one.

There once was a cow that smelled like manure.
Not the cow. Oh, no! I want the dog story instead.
I'm afraid I don't know that one.

There once was a rat that hunted a cat.
Not the rat. Oh, no! I want the dog story instead.
I'm afraid I don't know that one.

There once was an elephant that wore a spotted suit.
Not the elephant. Oh, no! I want the dog story instead.
I'm afraid I don't know that one.

There once was an ox that came and left.
Not the ox. Oh, no! I want the dog story instead.
I'm afraid I don't know that one.

There once was a sheep that always came in first.
Not the sheep. Oh, no! I want the dog story instead.
I'm afraid I don't know that one.

There once was a hyena that went to the movies.
Not the hyena. Oh, no! I want the dog story instead.
I'm afraid I don't know that one.

There once was an owl that walked with a limp.
Not the owl. Oh, no! I want the dog story instead.
I'm afraid I don't know that one.

There once was a dragon that lived in an oven.
Not the dragon. Oh, no! I want the dog story instead.
I'm afraid I don't know that one.

There once was a donkey that knew it all.
Not the donkey. Oh, no! I want the dog story instead.
I'm afraid I don't know that one.

There once was a snake that had only one tooth.
Not the snake. Oh, no! I want the dog story instead.
I'm afraid I don't know that one.

There once was a turkey that said "guzzle" and not "gobble."

Not the turkey. Oh, no! I want the dog story instead.

Ah! Now that one I know. . . .

There once was a dog with a very big heart; he was friends with the alligator that had only one foot, with the lion that had a great itch, with the pig that had a wonky snout, with the hen that hatched an idea, with the cow that smelled like manure, with the rat that hunted a cat, with the elephant that wore a spotted suit, with the ox that came and left, with the hyena that went to the movies, with the sheep that always came in first, with the owl that walked with a limp, with the dragon that lived in the oven, with the donkey that knew it all, with the snake that had only one tooth, and with the turkey that said "guzzle" and not "gobble."

(But what the little kid liked most of all was to count to three and say . . .)

Go on, Daddy! Tell me again!

There once was a dog . . .

Adélia Carvalho was born in Penafiel, Portugal, in 1969. She studied early childhood education and has worked as a teacher, often encouraging exchanges between writers and illustrators. In 2010, she launched the publishing company Tcharan together with the illustrator Marta Madureira. Since 2008, she has been writing and telling stories to children. All her books have been included in Portuguese National Reading Plan. *There Once Was a Dog* is her first picture book for NorthSouth Books.

João Vaz de Carvalho was born in Portugal in 1958. He is one of Portugal's best-known children's book illustrators. He has been awarded numerous prizes at home and abroad. He won first prize in the Biennale Illustration 2005 in Portugal. Through his pencil drawings and colorful paintings he creates wondrous adventures from the past and present. *There Once Was a Dog* is her first picture book for NorthSouth Books.

Make up a story about your favorite animal.

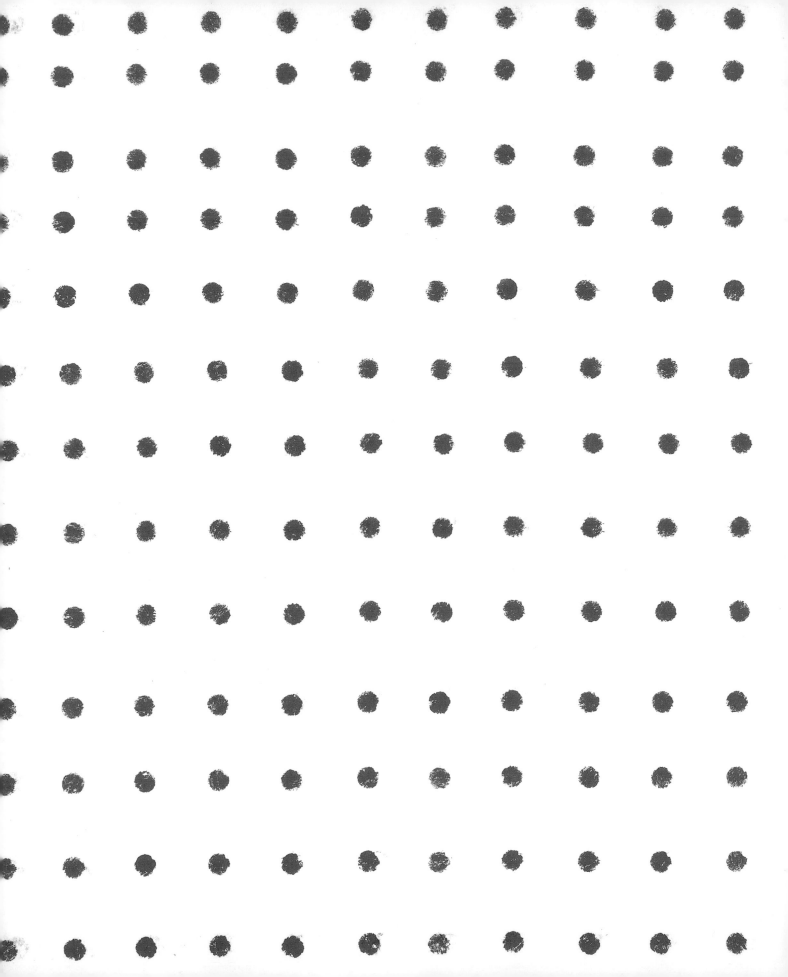